Famous Myths and Legends of the World

Myths and Legends of

AFRICA

WORLD
BOOK

a Scott Fetzer company
Chicago
www.worldbook.com

World Book, Inc.
180 North LaSalle Street
Suite 900
Chicago, Illinois 60601
USA

For information about other World Book publications, visit our website at **www.worldbook.com** or call **1-800-967-5325.**

Library of Congress Cataloging-in-Publication Data

Myths and legends of Africa.
    pages cm. -- (Famous myths and legends of the world)
    Summary: "Myths and legends from Africa. Features include information about the history and culture behind the myths, pronunciations, lists of deities, word glossary, further information, and index"--Provided by publisher.
    Includes index.
    ISBN 978-0-7166-2631-2
    1. Mythology, African--Juvenile literature. 2. Legends--Africa--Juvenile literature. I. World Book, Inc. II. Series: Famous myths and legends of the world.
    BL2400.M97 2015
    398.2096--dc23
                                2015014758

Set ISBN: 978-0-7166-2625-1
E-book ISBN: 978-0-7166-2643-5 (EPUB3)

Printed in China by PrintWORKS Global Services, Shenzhen, Guangdong
2nd printing May 2016

Writer: Scott A. Leonard

Staff for World Book, Inc.
Executive Committee
President: Jim O'Rourke
Vice President and Editor in Chief: Paul A. Kobasa
Vice President, Finance: Donald D. Keller
Vice President, Marketing: Jean Lin
Director, International Sales: Kristin Norell
Director, Human Resources: Bev Ecker

Digital
Director of Digital Products Development: Erika Meller
Digital Products Coordinator: Matthew Werner

Editorial
Manager, Annuals/Series Nonfiction: Christine Sullivan
Managing Editor, Annuals/Series Nonfiction:
    Barbara Mayes
Administrative Assistant: Ethel Matthews
Manager, Indexing Services: David Pofelski
Manager, Contracts & Compliance
    (Rights & Permissions): Loranne K. Shields

Manufacturing/Production
Manufacturing Manager: Sandra Johnson
Production/Technology Manager: Anne Fritzinger
Proofreader: Nathalie Strassheim

Graphics and Design
Senior Art Director: Tom Evans
Coordinator, Design Development and Production:
    Brenda Tropinski
Senior Designers: Matthew Carrington,
    Isaiah W. Sheppard, Jr.
Media Researcher: Rosalia Calderone
Manager, Cartographic Services: Wayne K. Pichler
Senior Cartographer: John M. Rejba

Staff for Brown Bear Books Ltd
Managing Editor: Tim Cooke
Editorial Director: Lindsey Lowe
Children's Publisher: Anne O'Daly
Design Manager: Keith Davis
Designer: Mike Davis
Picture Manager: Sophie Mortimer

CONTENTS

Traditional drumming, dancing, and singing, often in colorful costumes, are an important part of African life for both religious and social purposes.

The Dancer (1998), oil on canvas by Tilly Willis; Private Collection (Bridgeman Images)

Note to Readers:

Phonetic pronunciations have been inserted into the myths and legends in this volume to make reading the stories easier and to give the reader some of the flavor of the African cultures the stories represent. See page 64 for a pronunciation key.

The myths and legends retold in this volume are written in a creative way to provide an engaging reading experience and approximate the artistry of the originals. Many of these stories were not written down but were recited by storytellers from generation to generation. Even when some of the stories came to be written down they likely did not feature phonetic pronunciations for challenging names and words! We hope the inclusion of this material will improve rather than distract from your experience of the stories.

Some of the figures mentioned in the myths and legends in this volume are described on page 60 in the section "Deities of Africa." In addition, some unusual words in the text are defined in the Glossary on page 62.

INTRODUCTION

Africa is the second-largest continent in area and in population, after Asia. Although Africa consists of 54 independent countries and several other political units, it has several hundred ethnic groups, each with its own language or dialect and way of life.

Since the earliest times, people have told stories to try to explain the world in which they lived. These stories are known as myths. Myths try to answer such questions as, How was the world created? Who were the first people? Where did the animals come from? Why does the sun rise and set? Why is the land devastated by storms or drought? Today, people often rely on science to answer many of these questions. But in earlier times—and in some parts of the world today—people explained natural events using stories about gods, goddesses, spirits of nature, and heroes.

Myths are different from folk tales and legends. Folk tales are fictional stories about people or animals. Most of these tales are not set in any particular time or place, and they begin and end in a certain way. For example, many English folk tales begin with the phrase "Once upon a time" and end with "They lived happily ever after." Legends are set in the real world, in the present or the historical past. They distort the truth but are based on real people or events.

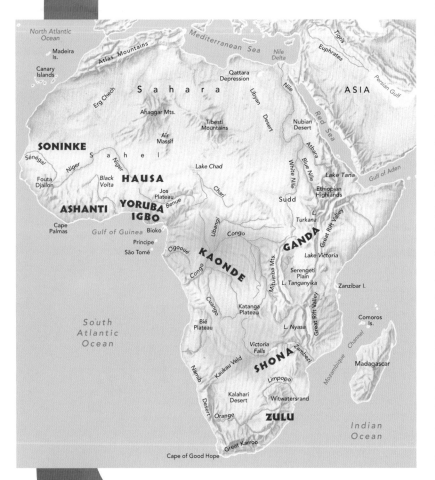

Myths, in contrast, typically tell of events that have taken place in the remote past. Unlike legends, myths have also played—and often continue to play—an important role in a society's religious life. Although legends may have religious themes, most are not religious in nature. The people of a society may tell folk tales and legends for amusement, without believing them. But they usually consider their myths sacred and completely true.

Most myths concern *divinities* or *deities* (divine beings). These divinities have powers far greater than those of any human being. At the same time, however, many gods, goddesses, and heroes of mythology have human characteristics. They are guided by such emotions as love and jealousy, and they may experience birth and death. Mythological figures may even look like human beings. Often, the human qualities of a culture's divinities reflect that society's ideals. Good gods and goddesses have the qualities a society admires, and evil ones have the qualities it dislikes. In myths, the actions of these divinities influence the world of humans for better or for worse.

Myths can sometimes seem very strange. They sometimes seem to take place in a world that is both like our world and unlike it. Time can go backward and forward, so it is sometimes difficult to tell in what order events happen. People may be dead and alive at the same time.

The World of the Igbo, page 30

The World of the Zulu, page 48

Myths were originally passed down generation to generation by word of mouth. Partly for this reason, there are often different versions of the same story. Many myths across cultures share similar themes, such as a battle between good and evil. But the myths of a society generally reflect the landscape, climate, and society in which the storytellers lived. Myths tell people about their distant history. They show people how to behave in the world and find their way. As teaching tools, myths help to prepare children for adulthood.

A people's folklore includes its myths, legends, and traditional folk tales and songs. Folklore also includes customs and beliefs. Children learn about their folklore from teachers and older people in their society. Every society around the world has a folklore that is special to it.

Myths and Legends of Africa

Millions of Africans practice local traditional religions. There are hundreds of African traditional religions because each ethnic group has its own set of beliefs and practices. In general, however, local religions have many features in common. They explain how the universe was created and teach what is right and wrong. They define relationships between human beings and nature and between the young and the old. They give the reasons for human suffering and instruct people in how to live a good life and in how to avoid or lessen misfortune.

African traditional religions all recognize the existence of a supreme god. However, most African traditional religions emphasize that people should seek help by appealing to lesser gods or to the spirits of dead ancestors. People pray or offer sacrifices to the gods or the spirits to gain such things as good health or fertile land. Many religions conduct ceremonies to celebrate a person's passage from childhood to adulthood.

The more complex African religions include those of certain peoples of western Africa, such as the Dogon of Mali, the Yoruba of Nigeria, and the Ashanti of Ghana. The religions of these peoples include elaborate sets of beliefs about a supreme being and a *pantheon* (collection) of lesser gods. Women as well as men hold important religious positions in western Africa.

The World of the Soninke, page 40

Although many of the stories in this book appear simple at first glance, they are layered with meaning. Retellings of the stories often reveal new insights. By studying myths, we can learn how different societies have answered basic questions about the world and the individual's place in it. By examining myths, we can better understand the feelings and values that bind members of society into one group. We can also compare the myths of various cultures to discover how these cultures differ and how they resemble one another.

ANANSI Plays Dead

The Ashanti of Ghana tell this story to explain why spiders hide in dark corners. The tale also emphasizes how important it is to trust your neighbors.

One year, famine came—many plants in the fields dried up, and the cattle died. There was no food for sale in the market. But Anansi (uh NAHN see) the Spider owned a farm, so he and his family had enough to eat. Still, just hearing the word *famine* made Anansi hungry. So he figured out a way to have his family's crop all to himself.

Anansi told his wife he was not feeling well and that he would consult a woman in the village who could see the future. When he returned, he said, "It is terrible news! The seer says I will die soon." He added that the seer had said his dead body should be buried at the end of his field, near where the yams grew.

"Please bury me with a mortar and pestle, dishes, spoons, and cooking pots so I can look after myself in the after-life," Anansi said to his family.

A few days later, Anansi lay down on his mat, as though he was sick, and then pretended to die. His wife and sons buried him. But Anansi stayed in his grave only during daylight. At night, he crept from his grave, stole the best yams from his field, then cooked and ate them. When dawn came, he returned to his grave.

Soon Anansi's wife and sons noticed that someone was stealing their best yams. They prayed at Anansi's grave, "Anansi, please send your spirit to protect us or we will starve!" But each day more yams were missing. So Anansi's family made a figure from sticky gum and straw and placed it in the yam patch. "We soon will see who has been stealing our yams," they said.

That night, as Anansi crept from his grave, he was startled to see what looked like a person. "Hey!" shouted Anansi. "What are you doing in my field?" The person made no reply. "If you don't leave at once, I will beat you!" Anansi declared. Again, getting no reply, Anansi lost his temper and punched the person with his right fist. It stuck fast to the person!

"O-ho! So you want to play!?" Anansi struck the person with his left fist. It, too, stuck fast. "If you don't let me go and leave immediately, I will beat you and take you before the chief of the village!"

But again the person remained silent. So Anansi kicked him. His foot, too, stuck fast. Furious, Anansi flailed about until he was completely stuck to the person and unable to move.

In the morning, Anansi's wife and sons saw him stuck to the straw figure and understood everything. They pried Anansi loose and marched him to the village to stand before the chief. Their neighbors stopped their work to laugh. Anansi was so ashamed, he fled to the nearest house and hid in the rafters. To this day, Anansi hides in dark corners to avoid people.

The World of
THE ASHANTI

The Ashanti are among the peoples of the west African countries of Ghana and Côte d'Ivoire who speak the Akan language. The Ashanti call themselves Asante. Ashanti is also the name of 1 of 10 local administrative regions that make up Ghana. Historically, Ashanti was a powerful military and political state, and Asante influence extended far beyond the boundaries of modern Ghana. Today, Ashanti includes only about 10 percent of Ghana's land area, but it ranks as the most populous region of the country.

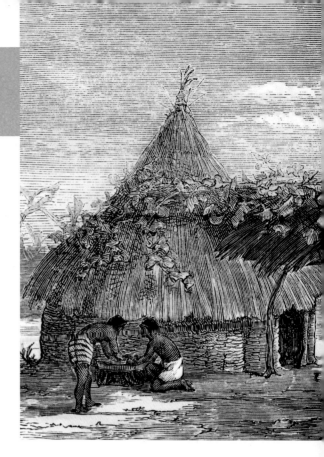

An Ashanti *shaman* (person believed to have magical powers) covers himself with white powder during a ritual dance. The powder symbolizes his spiritual death and purification. The Ashanti believed it was possible to learn what the future might hold by consulting the spirit world through a practice called *adebisa* (divination). Individuals consulted seers about marriage, a newborn's personality, the advisability of starting a new business, and whether one's ancestors in the afterlife required anything. No Ashanti chief would consider moving a village, waging war, or even going on a hunt without consulting a seer.

ASHANTI AFTERLIFE

Ashanti culture placed great significance on funerals. Traditionally, people attending funerals wore special garments consecrated for funerals and funeral processions. The Ashanti also traditionally presented "gifts" to the dead person, including pottery, figurines, smoking pipes, and such personal objects as stools, toiletries, and family heirlooms. People were usually buried with their prized possessions. A person's social status was measured by the number of those marching in the funeral procession and the number of gifts buried with him or her.

The Ashanti traditionally lived in villages similar to this group of huts shown in a drawing from the 1800's. The village was the center of Ashanti life. The village was the focus of important sacred ceremonies in which everyone was expected to take part.

SPIDER MAN

Anansi (uh NAHN see), who often appears in African tales as a spider, is a trickster, a common character in myths. Tricksters usually behave on impulse and have big appetites. Tales usually show tricksters as lazy and greedy, opportunists and thieves, manipulators and taboo-breakers. Although they play tricks on others, those tricks often backfire on them. Tricksters serve as moral counterexamples. That is, they show how *not* to behave.

Otumfuo Osei Tutu II, the Asantehene (king) of the Ashanti, sits among members of his court at Manhyia Palace, his seat of government and residence in Kumasi, Ghana.

An Ashanti woman weaves a special ceremonial cloth called kente (KEHN tay) cloth. Kente cloth is woven in narrow strips about 4 inches (10 centimeters) wide that are sewn together. The cloth's brightly colored patterns and strong geometrical shapes have different sacred meanings. Kente cloth was originally worn only by Ashanti kings and only for sacred occasions. Today, Kente cloth is more widely worn and has become a worldwide symbol of African heritage.

AJA, AJAPA,
and the Yams

For the Yoruba of Nigeria and Benin, this story about a cunning dog emphasizes how important it is for farmers to work to obtain enough food for the community.

Aja the Dog had no money. His wife was skinny, and his children were even skinnier. So Aja came up with a plan. He would steal yams from his neighbors' farms. But he would steal only a few and never more than once from the same farm until he'd visited all the farms. After all, thought Aja, no one will miss a yam or two.

Soon Ajapa the Tortoise noticed that Aja and his wife and children had grown plump and healthy.

"Aja, my friend," said Ajapa, "you are looking prosperous. What is your secret?"

Aja knew that if he told Ajapa the truth, everything would be ruined. But he also knew that if he didn't tell Ajapa, he'd never again know a moment's peace.

"If I tell you," Aja said, "you must promise to follow my instructions and keep what you see to yourself."
"Of course!" said Ajapa.

That night, Aja and Ajapa met on the road near a large yam farm. Aja quickly pulled up three large yams, enough to feed his wife and children for two days. But Ajapa was nowhere to be seen. "Ajapa!" hissed Aja, "We must hurry or the farmer will catch us!"

"In a minute," answered Ajapa, none too quietly, "I don't have enough just yet."

After what seemed like hours, Ajapa staggered out of the yam patch, struggling under the weight of a bag so full of yams he could hardly walk. "What are you doing!?" Aja cried in alarm. "I told you to take only what you need for one day! This farmer will never rest until he catches the one who took so many of his yams!"

"In trouble for one yam, in trouble for a lot of yams. What's the difference?" insisted Ajapa. "Now, are you going to help me with my burden or not, old friend?"

"I'm not waiting around to be caught!" cried Aja. And so he fled with his few yams back to his house. Behind him, he could hear his friend calling out, "Aja, Aja, come back and help me carry these yams!"

Aja hid his stolen yams among the trees near his house. Then, bursting through the door into his home, he cried, "Wife! Trouble is coming! Build a fire and bring me two eggs!"

Sure enough, not long after, two men stood outside Aja's door. "Aja! Come out! The Oba (AW buh) commands your presence immediately!" Aja's wife flung

14

open the door. "How dare you shout at my poor husband? He is practically at death's door and needs to rest."

The chief's men entered the hut and found Aja huddled in a blanket, shivering near the fire. He was covered in sweat, and when they approached him, he moaned and broke one of the eggs in his mouth so that he appeared to vomit!

"Come with us, Aja. The Oba commands it," they said. In a weak voice, Aja said, "As you can see, I am quite sick. But the Oba must be obeyed."

The chief's men laid the seemingly frail Aja in a wagon and brought him before the Oba. "There you are," said the Oba. "That thief Ajapa has leveled serious charges against you. He says that you thought up a scheme to steal from your neighbors!"

"As you can see, Oba, I am terribly sick," Aja moaned, "and have been so for days. I can hardly walk, never mind dig around in my neighbors' fields!" "It is so," confirmed the Oba's men.

"LIAR!" shouted Ajapa. "You were with me stealing yams just last night!" Ajapa attempted to grab his friend. At that moment, Aja broke the other egg in his mouth and spit it right in Ajapa's face.

Worried that he would also get sick, the Oba cried, "Take that poor wretch back home! And clean up that mess!" "As for you," he said, pointing at Ajapa, "those who steal from their neighbors and friends can never be trusted. You are banished to the forest. If you ever return to this village, you will be killed!"

This is why Aja the Dog lives with men in the village, and Ajapa the Tortoise lives in the woods.

The Yoruba (YOH ru bah) make up an ethnic group living mainly in southwestern Nigeria, Benin, and Togo. Powerful Yoruba kingdoms, such as Ife (EE fay) and Oyo, flourished around 1300. Many Yoruba were brought to the Americas by the slave trade from the late 1400's to the 1800's. Yoruba culture imported by slaves has been a major influence on art, music, and religion in the Americas.

OBA, THE KING

The Yoruba word *oba* (AW buh), roughly translated, means *king.* The oba's role included religious and judicial duties as well as those of a more political nature. In rural areas, obas were usually tribal chieftains, but some ruled over widespread tribal confederations to which many people belonged. Upon taking office, obas wore tall crowns and veils over their faces to symbolize their heavenly authority and moral uprightness. No one was permitted to see the face behind the oba's veil, which created an aura of mystery and majesty.

The royal palace in Ketou, Benin, is the seat of the Yoruba kingdom of Ketou, a city-state founded in the 1400's. Today, Ketou is a political unit in Benin.

Yoruba religious belief is complex. Their supreme being is a *trinity* (three-part god) who includes Olodumare, the Creator; Olorun (oh loh ROON), the lord of heaven; and Olofi, who transmits prayers from Earth to heaven and the will of Olorun to Earth. The Yoruba also have hundreds of lesser "spirits" called *orishas* (oh REE shuhs). Aja and Ajapa are orishas, embodying certain qualities like cunning, greed, and laziness. Although these are negative qualities in themselves, they can teach people valuable, if painful, lessons about behavior that leads to a productive life with fewer conflicts with others.

A Yoruba figure called an ere ibeji is carved after one of a set of twins dies to hold the spirit of the dead twin. The mother of the twins clothes and feeds the ere ibeji to keep the spirit happy. If the second twin dies, the mother will have another ere ibeji created. The birthrate for twins among the Yoruba is the highest in the world. The Yoruba believe that twins bring their families good luck and prosperity.

A Nigerian woman peels the roots of bitter cassava, a *staple* (major) food for the Yoruba and many other peoples in tropical Africa. The cassava, or white yam, is an important source of carbohydrates. If not properly prepared, however, it produces toxic levels of cyanide, a poisonous substance, in the body. The Yoruba also eat *tubers* (thick, enlarged portions of a stem that usually grow underground), grains, and plantains, supplemented by fruits, vegetables, meat, and fish. The bitter cassava is a good crop because insects and rodents avoid it. It grows quickly in dense patches that yield many roots from a small area of land.

CHAMELEON OUTWITS THE SEA GODDESS

The Yoruba of Nigeria and Benin tell this myth to explain how Olorun became the chief of all the gods by tricking the sea goddess Olokun, who had tried to humiliate him.

The Lord God, Olorun (oh loh ROON), the Owner of Endless Space, King of the Sky, had two sons, Orunmilla (oh RUHN mee lah) and Obatala (ah BAH tah lah). Their realm overlooked the wild, watery world of Olokun (OH loh koon), the sea goddess.

Obatala thought Olokun's realm was dreary. There is no imagination, no living thing in all that water, he thought. To his father he said, "If there were land in the realm below, we powerful spirits and other living things could live there." Olorun said, "This is a difficult under-taking." "Nevertheless," replied Obatala, "I will accomplish it."

Obatala consulted his brother, Orunmilla, the One Who Knows Who Will Prosper. Orunmilla repeatedly cast 16 palm nuts onto a holy tray, adding one meaning to another. His ritual complete, Orunmilla said, "If the work is to succeed, you must descend to Olokun's watery wasteland on a golden chain. Take a snail shell full of sand, a white hen, a black cat, and a palm nut."

Obatala followed these instructions. Descending the golden chain, he felt the chill of Olokun's realm when he was only halfway down. Bravely, he pressed on until he reached the chain's end, but he still had not reached Olokun's watery world. In the chilly darkness, he heard the pounding surf and smelled the marshland's reek.

His brother's voice sounded from above, "The sand!" Obatala poured out the sand. He released the white hen, which began to scratch the sand in all directions. Wherever the sand landed became dry land. Hills, plains, and valleys took shape. When the land was formed, Obatala dropped from the golden chain to Earth and looked around. He named the spot Ife (EE fay).

Obatala planted the palm nut. Soon a tree grew, producing more nuts until vegetation surrounded Ife. But there was no other life. Obatala had only his black cat for company.

After some time, Olorun sent his trusted messenger Agemo (ah GEH maw) the Chameleon to see how Obatala was getting on. "As you can see," said Obatala, "there is land and palm trees, but this gloomy place needs light." Agemo reported this to Olorun. The great god created the sun and set it moving above what had once been Olokun's world.

Later, Obatala said, "It would be better if many people lived here." He worked hard, fashioning figures of people from clay and laying them in the sun to dry. Fatigue and heat overcame him. So he created palm wine and refreshed himself. The world softened, and the work became easier. But Obatala's fingers were clumsy. Many of his clay figures were misshapen in some way. But he did not notice and labored on.

When he finished, Obatala cried out, "I have made human beings, but only you can give them life, Sky Father!" Olorun breathed life into the figures, and they became flesh and blood. They built houses and planted fields, and Ife expanded. Satisfied, Obatala ascended the golden chain to heaven.

The sea goddess, Olokun, was unhappy that the heavenly spirits had invaded her private realm. She sent great waves to cover the land. Ife's people cried out to heaven, and Orunmilla, the One Who Knows Who Will Prosper—Olorun's eldest son—came to Earth. Through wisdom and magic, he stopped Olokun's attempt to destroy all that Obatala had built.

Olokun decided to humiliate Olorun. She was an expert at weaving and dyeing cloth, so she challenged Olorun to a contest. Olorun would certainly lose, but he could not refuse. Then he saw the solution. He instructed Agemo (ah GEH maw) the Chameleon and sent him to Olokun.

"The Owner of Sky greets you," said Agemo to Olokun. "He will accept your challenge only if your clothmaking is as magnificent as you say. Please show me your best work so I may report to him."

Olokun put on a shimmering green skirt. As Agemo admired it, his skin became the exact same color. She put on a sunset-colored skirt. Again, Agemo's skin matched it. Olokun put on a red skirt and Agemo turned red. The sea goddess put on a multicolored skirt, but Agemo reproduced it perfectly.

"If Olorun's messenger can match my most beautiful colors exactly, how much more skilled than I must the Sky King be," Olokun thought. "Offer greetings to the Owner of Sky for me, Agemo." she said. "Tell him Olokun acknowledges his greatness." And thus Olorun rules over everything and everyone.

The World of OLORUN

Ife (EE fay) was an important black African city-state founded around 950 by the Yoruba. Ife reached the height of its power about 1300. Scholars believe Ife prospered by controlling much of the slave, gold, and ivory trade along the lower Niger River. In the early 1500's, Ife began to decline as trade shifted from inland routes to the coast. Ife culture is known for its outstanding sculptures of *terra cotta* (baked clay) and brass, most of which date from the 1100's to the 1400's. Today, Ife is a city in southwestern Nigeria. The Yoruba view the city as a holy place and believe it was the creation point of the universe.

← Dressed in traditional clothing, a Yoruba woman poses with her children. Yoruba myths and proverbs emphasize the importance of the family in Yoruba society. The family is the basis of social organization, everyday life, and socializing. Families are grouped into larger clans, which trace their descent back to a common ancestor. Traditionally the Yoruba were *polygamous*—that is, men had more than one wife. Today, polygamy is much less common, but some men marry a second wife if they do not have a child with their first wife.

THE OONI

The Ooni (traditional ruler) of Ife (EE fay) claims descent from the god Obatala (ah BAH tah lah). The current Ooni, Olubuse II, traces his lineage back over 2,000 years. Traditionally, the Ooni of Ife has had great status as the high priest and custodian of the Yoruba's most important city. Today, the Ooni participates in the most important celebrations in Ife's busy religious calendar.

Men wearing colorful headdresses that include a mask and veil dance at a Yoruba festival called Gelede. The festival celebrates the importance of women, including female ancestors and the female elders of the community. Gelede is entertaining, but it is also meant to educate the watchers and encourage their worship of the gods.

BEST FRIENDS

To the Yoruba, a best friend is second in importance only to family members. The Yoruba refer to a best friend as "friend not-see-not-sleep." That suggests that best friends need to see each other every day. A best friend is so important that a person who is dying tries to share his last wishes with that person.

← Court drummers play at a ceremony for the ruler of the Yoruba town of Ede in Nigeria. Drumming, dancing, and singing are an important part of Yoruba life. There are songs and dances for such special occasions as coronations but also for more everyday events. Fishers and other groups have their own songs and dances. Drumming is used in religious ceremonies because it is thought to help worshipers communicate with the gods.

A head titled "Olokun," cast in bronze, is an example of the fine sculptures for which the Yoruba are known. Figures and heads in bronze, brass, stone, and terra cotta usually represent orishas (oh REE shuhs), which were seen as physical manifestations, or appearances in the world, of the gods. In the past, virtually all Yoruba art was produced to honor the many gods.

SEIDU the Brave

The Hausa tell this story as a warning to men who are proud and boastful.

There once was a man named Seidu (say doo) from a place called Golo. After every hunt, Seidu returned boasting, "I alone chased the lion and elephant. They fled before my spear. I am the bravest hunter!" "Did no one else have success in the hunt?" asked Ladi, his wife. "Yes," Seidu replied, "but they succeeded only because I am so fearless and chased down the animals for them to kill."

When enemies approached the village, Seidu joined the other men to defend their families and homes. Afterward, Seidu said, "The enemies fled from my spear. I am the bravest of all warriors."

One day, the village women wished to attend a funeral in a nearby village. But the men were busy and could not accompany them. "Seidu," said Ladi. "You are the bravest of men. Please go with us as we travel to the funeral."

"I never hear about my bravery," complained Seidu, "until I am needed. But I will go."

And so they went. But enemies lurked in the forest. "See that man strutting with that group of women? Let's put fear into him." So the enemies surrounded Seidu and the women, their spears upraised.

Frowning at Seidu's wife, the enemy leader demanded, "What is your name?" "Ladi," she replied. "Ladi is an honored name in our village. We will not harm you," said the enemy.

The enemy leader demanded to know each woman's name. Seeing how well things turned out for Seidu's wife, each said her name was Ladi. At last the leader turned to Seidu. "You there, Rooster, with all these hens—what is your name?"

"Ladi," replied Seidu. "Ladi is a woman's name in our village," scoffed the enemy captain. "Do men go by women's names in your village?" "Appearances are deceiving," replied Seidu. "I am actually a woman dressed as a man!"

The warriors laughed themselves sick. "It is not so," objected Ladi. "My husband maligns himself. He is Seidu, bravest of men." The enemy leader said, "They say Seidu is the bravest of men. Is that so?" "It is no longer so," answered Seidu. "I once was known as the bravest of men. I am now only the bravest of my village."

Having had their fun, the enemies released Seidu and the women. When they got home, everyone made fun of Seidu, calling him Ladi.

Ashamed, Seidu could no longer bear to leave his hut. Finally, he asked his wife to take a message to the villagers. "Once, I was Seidu, the bravest of all men. From now on, I am Seidu, no braver than anyone else." And so the people stopped making fun of Seidu, and life in the village returned to normal.

The World of THE HAUSA

The Hausa (HOW sah) live in West Africa. There about 7 million Hausa, who make up an important cultural and political group in northern Nigeria and southern Niger. Although most Hausa are Muslims, a traditional religion is still practiced in many rural areas.

Houses made from grass or dried mud with thatched roofs line a roadway in a traditional Hausa farming village. Such villages are home to between 2,000 and 12,000 people.

TRADITIONAL RELIGION

Older traditional Hausa religion features a belief in thousands of spirits or "winds" called *iskoki*. The iskoki can be divided into two groups: the farm spirits and the bush spirits. Farm spirits are considered easier to contact and more likely to help those who sacrifice to them than are the untamable bush spirits.

A boy displays facial scarification still practiced by some Hausa clans. The patterns of scars communicate complex messages about the individual and his or her identity.

A Hausa woman spins cotton fiber to make thread. Women do not have a prominent role in Hausa society. They are usually confined to their homes, where they perform domestic tasks. Hausa girls have fewer educational opportunities than boys. Women are often referred to in terms of their relationships to men—that is, women are described as someone's daughter, wife, mother, or widow.

A Hausa emir (uh MIHR), or chief, (front) and fellow nobles display their high social status with their colorful, highly ornamented clothing and headdresses and horses with decorative bridles. The Hausa became famous in the Midde Ages (A.D. 400 to the 1400's) for their *indigo* (blue) robes and Arabian horses. Hausa society divides men into chiefs and commoners. The chiefs and nobles are expected to display their wealth, religious devotion, and political authority.

WHY DEATH IS PERMANENT

Chukwu, honored by the Igbo as the creator, did not want death to be permanent. But two unreliable messengers—Dog and Sheep—failed Chukwu and he did not get his wish.

Chukwu (CHOOK woo) created all things—gods and spirits, Earth and sky, and the people and animals living on Earth. Chukwu was good and kind. He felt sad whenever anyone died.

So he told Dog, his trusted messenger, to go to Earth and speak his holy word: "From now on, do not bury those who die! Place all who die on the ground. Cover them in wood ash. The next day, the dead will live again!"

Dog began his journey down to Earth to deliver Chukwu's word. But the road between heaven and Earth is long, and eventually Dog grew tired and hungry. A scent tickled his nose.

Following the scent, he peeked inside an old woman's house and saw a bone with meat still clinging to it. He snatched it and ran some way off to devour his meal. Soon, Dog forgot all about the message he was to deliver.

When Dog did not return, Chukwu sent Sheep to deliver his message to the people. And so Sheep began his journey down to Earth. But the road between heaven and Earth is long, and, smelling sweet green grass alongside the road, Sheep soon began grazing.

Suddenly, Sheep remembered his important errand, but he forgot the details of the message. Coming to where the people were, Sheep announced, "Chukwu, the Mighty, tells you to bury your dead underground!"

Soon afterward, Dog also remembered why he had come to Earth. He ran as fast as he could to deliver his message. "Hear the word of Chukwu, our Creator! Place your dead upon the ground and cover them with wood ash. After a day, the dead will live again!" "We don't believe you," the people said. "Sheep has already delivered Chukwu's word that we are to bury our dead."

To this day, Dog is hated by humans. If only he had delivered Chukwu's word immediately instead of stopping to fill his stomach! If he had, people would never know death.

The World of
THE IGBO

The Igbo live in southeastern Nigeria in a region often ➡ called Igboland. They occupy highland plains, coastal areas, and tropical forests and valleys along the Niger River. Most Igbo make their living as farmers. Their most important crops are yams, cassava, and taro. (The thick root of the cassava plant and the underground starchy stem of the taro plant are eaten as food.) Most Igbo adopted Christianity in the 1800's and early 1900's, when Nigeria was controlled by the United Kingdom. However, many Igbo maintain their traditional African religion from before that time.

People wearing ceremonial clothes celebrate the arrival of the new year in an Igbo village. For the Igbo, the textiles worn for such occasions have much social value. Cloth once served not only as clothing but also as a marker of social rank and even money. Igbo women specialize in weaving *akwete* (water) cloth, which requires great skill and imagination. Woven on a machine called a loom, akwete cloth features colorful patterns said to be directly inspired by the gods. For this reason, designs are never duplicated. Each individual design dies with its weaver.

BOTCHED MESSAGE

A number of African cultures tell stories about unreliable messengers who doom human beings to death. For example, the Zulu say the Moon, who "dies" and is reborn each month, sent the garbled message by way of a chameleon. Other cultures say it was a rabbit, whose split upper lip is the result of being struck on the nose for getting the message wrong.

Igbo chiefs attend the funeral of famous Nigerian author Chinua Achebe in 2013. The leading chief (right in photo) wears a photo of Achebe, an Igbo. Traditional Igbo burial customs depended on the age, gender, and rank of the dead person. The prominent dead were dressed in their best garments and propped up on stools for a day so that others might honor the dead by offering animal sacrifices. Children were buried in hidden places during the early morning or late night. A male commoner's body was usually buried outside his house. A female commoner's body was buried in a garden or a field owned by her father. Today, most burials occur in the Western way, but traditional customs are still common.

Striking colors decorate an *ikenga*, one of the most common carvings made by Igbo artists. Such statues, which represent warriors, are an expression of personal identity—including the influence of ancestors and the gods—for Igbo men of high status. The statues are often kept in personal shrines in Igbo homes. The sword carried in the right hand, the staff held in the left hand, the horns, and the elaborate headdress are typical features of ikenga.

IGBO GOVERNMENT

For the most part, traditional Igbo government consisted of democratically selected assemblies. This system promised relative equality for all Igbo people, though reverence for elders usually meant that councils of elders occupied specially designated roles. Many other African nations were organized under the rule of royal dynasties, lines or rulers belonging to the same family.

THE CRUEL MOTHER

A mother who treats her daughter badly receives a more terrible punishment than she had ever imagined in this West African tale.

Once a woman gave birth to a girl who grew into a beautiful young woman. The daughter was obedient, hard working, and gentle, but her mother found only fault in her. She scolded and beat her daughter, often shaming her in public.

Eventually, the daughter was promised as wife to a young man. "Mother," said the daughter, "won't you please buy the clothes, jewelry, and things needed for my wedding day?" "The matter is in hand," her mother lied. "I'm saving all you need in a special basket." And the lie grew. Often, her mother would falsely announce she had added items to the basket.

At last the young woman's wedding day arrived. "Mother," she said, "may I now see what you've placed in the basket?" Her mother laid the basket at her feet, but when the daughter opened it, she found only leaves and string made to look like jewelry and other ornaments.

"Here is your reward! You lazy, headstrong girl!" crowed the mother. "I'm glad we will no longer live together!"

The beautiful young woman began to cry. Tears poured down her cheeks. Her eyes grew red, her face pale. And still she cried, until she began to sink into the earth.

Only when the girl was waist-deep in the ground did her mother notice. "My daughter, my daughter!" she cried. "I was wrong! Please come back to me! I will buy you dresses and rings! I will buy you beads! I will give you everything!"

But her daughter sank deeper. Soon only her hair was visible. Kneeling in grief, the mother clutched her daughter's hair and begged her to return.

But it was too late. The daughter was gone. This is why we should never be cruel to our children.

The World of WEST AFRICA

West Africa is made up of some 20 countries, including such prosperous nations as Côte d'Ivoire, Ghana, Liberia, and Nigeria. Once home to a number of native empires, the region became a major hub of the African slave trade in the mid-1400's. By the early 1900's, France and the United Kingdom controlled nearly all of West Africa. But by the mid-1970's, all the countries of the region had gained their independence.

A young Nigerian bride is blessed by her grandmother on her wedding day (below). In West Africa, the bond between generations of a family is very important. The family elders give younger members of the family advice about their careers and social lives.

FOLKTALES

Africa's folk tales are often presented orally and serve many functions. They especially focus on social values, etiquette, behavioral codes, kinship relations, marriage, and social organization. One common kind of tale involves a parent willing to let someone marry his or her daughter only if that person is able to perform a seemingly impossible task. Usually the successful suitor in these stories originally appears weak or insignificant. Another common type is the "dilemma tale," which exposes a problem, develops it, and then asks the audience to discuss it.

At weddings in Nigeria and other parts of West ➡ Africa, the bride, groom, and their parents share a kola nut to symbolize the union of their families. The nut is the seed of several kinds of evergreen trees that are native to West Africa. The nut is traditionally used to make medicine, so it is seen as a symbol that a couple will always take care of one another.

In the story "The Cruel Mother," the daughter hopes to collect jewelry, clothing, and other things for her wedding. In many traditional societies, a wife is also expected to bring a dowry to a marriage. This is usually a payment by the wife's family to the family of her husband. The payment can be made in money, goods, or property. It is a form of compensation to the husband's family for having to support the new wife.

Female guests at a wedding in the West African country of Niger stand in a circle, singing and playing drums, while male guests ride their camels around them to the rhythm of the drums. In West Africa, a wedding is seen as the union of two families. The celebrations sometimes last several days and include races, games, singing, dancing, and elaborate feasts.

A bold pattern decorates a coil basket from Sierra Leone. Baskets woven from grass are widely used in West Africa to store not just special items—like the wedding clothes in the story—but also such everyday items as rice. The grass is woven into thick cables that are then wound up to make a basket. Baskets were also important farming tools that were used to *winnow* (separate) the *chaff* (strawlike bits) from the rice at harvest time.

GASSIRE
and the Lute that Sang

The great warrior Gassire longed to take his father's place as king. But in order to do so, he first had to learn how to sing the dausi, the great songs of the Soninke people.

Wagadu (wah gah doo), the great city, has existed under four names. It fell four times, each time because of a different human weakness. This is the story of the first time Wagadu fell.

Vanity caused the first fall. In those days, the city was ruled by King Nganamba Fasa (nah gah NAHM bah FAH sah). His eldest son, Gassire, had eight grown sons. Every day, Gassire rode into battle, a mighty hero carrying fearsome weapons. Every night, he listened as the men praised his deeds. But he cared little for their words. Instead he asked himself, "When will Nganamba die? When will I be king?"

Gassire's rage and impatience grew until he could not sleep. He could practically taste his longing for his father's sword

and shield! One night, he sprang from his bed to consult the wise man. "Kiekorro!" demanded Gassire. "When will my father, Nganamba, die, leaving his sword and shield to me?"

"Alas, Gassire," replied the old man, "Nganamba will indeed die, but he will not leave you his sword and shield. Instead, when you hear the partridge sing and understand its words, you will become the poet of your people. But Wagadu, the great city, will be lost!" "How," asked Gassire, "can Wagadu be lost when her heroes always triumph?"

The next day, Gassire's rage knew no limit. He commanded his soldiers to stay behind while he faced their enemy alone. He mowed them down like a scythe cuts grass, forcing the survivors to cast aside their spears and flee.

"The Fasa are mighty heroes!" Gassire's men sang that night. "Gassire has always been greatest among the Fasa! But today Gassire was greater than Gassire!" And yet Gassire was unhappy. He did not sit and feast with the men. He withdrew into the fields outside the city. There he heard a partridge singing and understood its meaning perfectly.

"Hear the words I sing" called the bird. "Hear my deeds! All creatures must die and rot. Heroes and kings are buried and forgotten. But my dausi, the song of my battles, shall never die! My song will be sung again and again, outliving heroes and kings! May my deeds be worthy of song!"

Gassire ran to Kiekorro. "Old man!" cried Gassire. "I heard a partridge sing its deathless song. Tell me, can men also know the deathless song?" Kiekorro replied, "It was said that in ancient times, the Fasa's enemies struck fear into our ancestors' hearts with such songs. You, Gassire, will become the poet of your people, but Wagadu will be lost." "Wagadu can go to blazes," said Gassire.

Gassire commanded an artisan to make him a lute (loot), but the instrument produced no sound. "What's this?" demanded Gassire. "This lute makes no sound!"

"A lute is only a piece of wood until it has a heart," said the artisan. "Carry this piece of wood on your back into battle. Only after it hears the ring of your sword will it have a heart to sing. Only when it feels your pain and tastes the blood of your blood will its song live on in the heart of your people. But Wagadu will still be lost." "Wagadu can go to blazes," said Gassire.

Gassire spoke to his eight sons. "Fight valiantly! Our sword strokes will no longer echo and be gone but will live forever in our people's song."

For seven days, Gassire strapped his lute to his back and went into battle alongside a different son. Although all of his sons were skilled warriors, each day Gassire returned bearing a slain son on his shoulder. The son's blood—the blood of Gassire's blood—soaked the instrument strapped to his back.

When at last only Gassire's youngest son was left alive, Wagadu's leaders said,

"Enough! We are willing to fight when necessary, but life matters more than fame. Go from the city. Take what remains of your family with you."

But, even days later, in the wilderness, Gassire could not rest. Late one night, he heard his lute singing. It sang in Gassire's voice the song of his people. As the great song rang out for the first time, King Nganamba died. And when the song rang out for the first time, Gassire's rage melted.

As the singing continued, Wagadu, the great city, disappeared for the first time, sleeping for generations before reawakening.

The Soninke (soh NIHNG kay) people of West Africa founded and ruled the Ghana (GAH nuh) Empire in what is now southeastern Mauritania and western Mali. The Ghana Empire (not to be confused with the modern country of Ghana) was an important black trading state from about the A.D. 300's to the mid-1000's. Today, the Soninke people also live in Gambia, Guinea-Bissau, and Senegal. There they grow millet and rice and raise livestock. In recent decades, a number of Soninke have migrated to Paris in search of work.

WAGADU

The story "Gassire and the Lute that Sang" suggests that the search for glory in battle brought an end to an early phase of the Ghana Empire. In contrast, European epics celebrate the great and often bloody deeds of such heroes as Achilles (uh KIHL eez), Ulysses (yoo LIHS eez), and Aeneas (ih NEE uhs).

Traditional Soninke society consisted of three main classes. They were the *hooro* (nobility and freemen), *naxamala* (workers, known as "dependent men"), and *komo* (slaves or servants). Kingship was hereditary, so only members of a royal house could become a ruler. However, other hooro, such as warriors (above) and nobles, had much influence over the king. Within the dependent class, smiths had the highest status because they made weapons of war and jewelry, important items in traditional culture.

THE DAUSI

The dausi was a cycle, or collection, of West African epic songs or stories. Epics are long narrative poems. Almost all epics tell about the heroic deeds of divine beings and people in war or travel. Many epics tell how a nation or people began. Epics date back to prehistoric times. The earliest ones were sung by poets who accompanied themselves on a stringed instrument. These epics had no established text. The singers composed each line as they sang it, following the outline of a traditional tale.

The *ngoni* (ehng GOH nee), or African lute, is the most popular stringed instrument in West Africa. It comes in different sizes but is usually quite small. It is used by wandering singers called *griots* (gree OHS) to accompany their songs about the history of their peoples.

The Soninke traditionally live in small houses with flat roofs and walls made from dried mud. Sometimes the walls have holes in them to allow cooling air to circulate (far left).

A Soninke woman applies a paste made from ground limestone to create a colorful geometric pattern on the outside wall of her home. In contrast, the interior of such a house is often relatively plain and sparsely furnished.

MAORI Allows the First Man to Go to Earth

The Shona of southern Africa tell this myth to explain how the world came into being. It also describes how an act of disobedience caused death to enter the world, and why the natural world is full of harmful and dangerous creatures.

Maori (MOW ree), the creator, made Mwuetsi, the moon, and placed him in the ocean's depths with a horn filled with oil. But Mwuetsi complained, begging Maori to let him live on land.

"If I do this," replied Maori, "you will experience death." Mwuetsi agreed and lived on the land, but it was empty. Again Mwuetsi complained. So Maori gave him a woman, Massassi (muh SAHS see), the morning star, endowing her with fire. "I give you this woman for two years," said Maori.

Mwuetsi and the woman lived in a cave. Massassi made fires and cooked meals. At first, Mwuetsi didn't know why Maori had sent the woman to him. One day, Mwuetsi opened his oil-horn, dipped a finger into it, and touched Massassi with the oil from his finger. The next morning, Massassi gave birth to the plants and trees that now cover Earth. Mwuetsi and Massassi grew food and built a home.

Two years later, as he said he would, Maori took Massassi away. Mwuetsi wept. "Who will start the fires? Who will gather wood? Who will cook the meals?"

After eight days, Maori said, "I warned you death would come. Nevertheless, I will give you Marongo (muh RAHNG goh), the evening star, for two years."

Marongo's belly soon grew large. On the first day, she gave birth to chickens, sheep, and goats. On the second, she gave birth to the eland and cattle. On the third morning, Marongo bore boys and girls, who by nightfall were full-grown. And so Mwuetsi became the Mambo, a great king ruling many people. Maori spoke, "It is enough. Cause no more to be born. Death is coming."

Mwuetsi and Marongo disobeyed Maori. The next morning, Marongo bore lions, leopards, snakes, and scorpions. "I warned you," said Maori.

After two years, as Mwuetsi slept, a snake bit him. He became very sick. The rain stopped. The lakes and rivers dried up. Many animals and people died.

Mwuetsi's children asked, "What can we do? Death devours the living!" Consulting the sacred objects, the children received an answer. "Mwuetsi must die and return to Maori in heaven."

So they sacrificed Mwuetsi to Maori. They also killed and buried Marongo with him. The people appointed a new king and the world flourished again.

The World of THE SHONA

The Shona (SHOH nuh) are the largest African ethnic group in the modern country of Zimbabwe (zihm BAH bway). The Shona are often called the Mashona. Most Shona in Zimbabwe are farmers and raise only enough food for their families. Their main crop, corn, is pounded into flour to make a dish called *sadza*.

↑

The city of Great Zimbabwe, now in ruins (above), in modern-day Zimbabwe, was the capital of a large empire ruled by the ancestors of the Shona. The wealth and power of the empire, which flourished from about A.D. 1100 to about 1450, came from vast herds of cattle that were kept for meat and milk. Two stone walls surround the Great Enclosure (top in photo). Between them rises a conical stone tower 30 feet (9 meters) high (hidden by trees). Nothing like the circular enclosure was built anywhere else in early Africa, and its purpose is still not fully understood.

High stone walls surround the Great Enclosure at Great Zimbabwe.

DIVINE KINGSHIP

Many African cultures believe in the concept of "divine kingship." Their myths and later political institutions and cultural beliefs suggest that the first king (usually the first man) was either directly fashioned by the creator or was in some sense the son of the creator. At death, the king passes into eternity to join the ancestors, and his successor is again considered to be the living image of the First Ancestor on Earth.

Shona musicians have played the *mbira*, or thumb piano, for centuries. It has a wooden soundboard with a row of *tines* (metal rods), which are tuned to make different sounds. The player makes the rods vibrate by pushing the ends down with the thumbs and the right index finger. The mbira is used to accompany stories, songs, and dances, and during religious ceremonies.

SACRED KING

"Maori Allows the First Man to Go to Earth" features the so-called "sacred king" *motif* (theme). It describes how the health and moral character of the king had a direct influence on the health and prosperity of the people. When the king loses his youthful vigor, he is sacrificed and a younger king takes his place. In this story, Mwuetsi becomes sick and so does his land; he must die for the land to be renewed. Although this motif appears in myths around the world, there is little evidence that the sacrifice of kings was ever a widespread practice.

A mourner wears a traditional mask made from feathers at the funeral of a Shona farmer.

A soapstone bird found at Great Zimbabwe, displays the artistry of Shona sculptors. (Soapstone is a soft rock composed mainly of the mineral talc.) To Shona carvers, stone—like everything else in the world—has a "life spirit" that influences what sculpture a particular stone will become. The sculptor's job is to "release" the spirit from the stone. The Shona believe carvings help to link the physical and the spiritual worlds.

UNCAMA'S
Journey to the Other World

Where do people go when they die? For the Zulu, the story of Uncama and the porcupine provided a hint about the Underworld.

Uncama dug and tended his corn garden carefully. But just as the corn started to grow ripe, he discovered a porcupine had eaten the choicest ears. Each day, Uncama woke to find that the porcupine had returned while he slept and taken the best ears of corn.

One morning, when dew lay thick on the ground, Uncama spied the porcupine's trail in the wet grass. "I will pursue this pest and kill it," he said.

Grabbing his weapons, he followed the porcupine's tracks until he came to its burrow. Uncama did not have a dog, so he entered the burrow himself, set on finding and killing the animal that was stealing food from the mouths of his wife and children.

At first, Uncama had difficulty seeing in the burrow's darkness. When his eyes adjusted, he became confused. He was in a world under the world, a place not unlike his own country. He walked for days. He passed a shallow lake. He crossed a river. He slept at night when he could go no farther.

Uncama eventually heard dogs barking and children playing. He saw smoke rising in the distance. He drew closer and saw a village. "What is this place!?" he exclaimed. "I followed a porcupine into a hole and found a village!"

Uncama suddenly became afraid. What if the villagers killed him because he was a stranger? He fled, retracing his steps until, days later, he emerged from the burrow and walked back to his house.

His wife screamed. "Uncama! You have returned!" Hearing the commotion, the villagers came running. Seeing Uncama, they clapped their hands and chanted the funeral song. "You were dead! So we buried your blankets and mat! Now you have returned!"

Uncama told them about his journey, but people kept their distance. For Uncama had changed. He was ugly now—hairy all over—and missing many teeth. People avoided him after that, as they avoid all those who visit the Underworld.

The Zulu (ZOO loo) live in the Republic of South Africa, mostly in the province of KwaZulu-Natal (KWA zoo loo nuh TAL). They make up the largest language group in that country. Many Zulu live in urban areas. Before British conquest in 1879, the Zulu were farmers and cattle herders. They lived in houses (left) made of finely matted reeds and straw. The houses have a low door, so that anyone going in or out has to bow. The houses were arranged in circles to form villages. The Zulu had a powerful monarch and a well-disciplined army. A Zulu man (left) wears the traditional warrior's dress—an animal skin decorated with colored beads, an animal-skin apron, and bands of furry goatskin around his arms and legs. His headdress is made from feathers and fur.

ANCESTOR WORSHIP

The Zulu have traditionally believed that a soul wanders Earth for a time after the death of the body. The soul must be "called back" to its homestead by a ceremony. According to traditional belief, the ancestors participate in everyday life, sometimes warning of trouble through dreams or intuitions. The guidance of ancestors is sought in difficult times and people show them respect through offerings. If the ancestors feel neglected, they may cause the living bad luck or illness.

The Zulu hung masks like this one (right) near the entrances to their homes. Such masks were not intended to look real. They were believed to offer protection from evil, sickness, and bad luck. The masks were also used to add drama to tribal festivals. People who wanted to confess secrets whispered them to masks, which could not reveal them. In the early 1900's, such European artists as Pablo Picasso and Amedeo Modigliani became fascinated with African masks and used similar shapes in their paintings.

The smallest unit of traditional Zulu society was the homestead, which usually included a man, his wife or wives, their young children, and other relatives. The family lodged in a number of houses surrounding a *kraal* (a fenced enclosure for cattle, right). The number of cattle a man owned was a measure of his wealth and political power. A man whose father had no cattle had little chance of marrying, because it was customary for a groom to give cattle to his wife's family when a marriage was arranged.

THE UNDERWORLD

A motif is a repeated theme or idea that occurs in all art forms. The underworld journey is a widespread motif. In *The Epic of Gilgamesh*, *The Odyssey*, and *The Aeneid*, the hero's successful journey to and from the underworld indicates his status as an exceptional human being. Many African stories feature ordinary people who enter burrows or caves only to find themselves in parallel worlds. Typically, those who return bring with them extraordinary knowledge, power, or special objects. Often they find the world has changed in their absence.

A woman wearing traditional Zulu dress weaves a straw carpet at a cultural village in South Africa. Zulu are skilled weavers. Zulu women traditionally wove the fabric for their own clothes, which were decorated with brightly colored beads. The design of the clothes reflected a woman's marital status: whether she was single, married, or a widow.

KINTU,
the First King

The Ganda people of
Uganda tell this story to
celebrate the deeds of
Kintu, their first king, who
brought their people
together.

When Kintu (kihn too) arrived on Earth, he had only a cow. He knew no other food. Some time later, Nambi (nam bee) and her brothers, the children of Gulu (goo loo), the Great God, came to Earth from heaven. Nambi fell in love with Kintu and wished to become his wife.

Nambi's family objected to this marriage. So her father, Gulu, proposed that Kintu be tested. "Take from Kintu his cow to see if he can live without the food she provides," he commanded.

At first, Kintu could not feed himself, but eventually he discovered that certain plants and herbs could be cooked and eaten. When Nambi realized that her brothers had stolen Kintu's cow, she returned to Earth and told him about it, inviting him to return with her to heaven to claim the beast. When Kintu arrived in heaven, he was surprised to see so many people, homes, and cattle.

When Nambi's brothers saw Kintu sitting with their sister, they complained to Gulu. "We must give this man more tests before we consent to any marriage," said Gulu. So they built Kintu a house, cooked a feast for 100 people, laid it on a long table, and said, "You must eat this feast all by yourself to prove you are Kintu."

Once Kintu ate his fill, he discovered a great hole in the floor and dumped the leftover food and beer into it. Nambi's brothers were astonished to see the entire meal gone and ran to Gulu, who said, "We will test this man further."

The brothers gave Kintu a copper ax, telling him that Gulu burned only stone for his fires. Accordingly, they took him to a rocky outcropping and said, "Chop logs from this for our father's fires or you are not Kintu."

Kintu realized that if he struck the stone, the blade would become dull and he would accomplish nothing. But he saw cracks in the rock, and so he broke off great pieces and delivered them to Gulu. The Great God could barely conceal his astonishment.

"Kintu," he said. "I am thirsty, but I drink only dew. Fill this pot and I will know you are truly great." Kintu took the pot to a field early in the morning and put it aside, trying to think of a way to fill it. But no ideas came to him. Discouraged, he picked up the pot—only to discover it was filled to the rim with dew!

When Gulu saw the filled pot, he exclaimed, "Kintu, you are truly a wonder! Take your cow from among the many here in heaven and Nambi shall be yours." At first Kintu was confused. Many cows in heaven resembled his own. But a bee flew near his ear. "Fear not," hummed the bee. "The cow upon whose head I land is your animal."

Nambi's brothers led Kintu from one herd to another, but when the bee did not land on them, he said, "My cow is not here." So the brothers took him to another herd, and this time the bee landed on a cow.

"This is my cow," Kintu said. And when the bee also settled on a young bull next to the cow, he added, "This is my cow's calf."

At last Gulu was satisfied. "Clearly, you have proved yourself resourceful enough to provide for my daughter. Nambi shall be your wife. But leave immediately! Do not return or Nambi's brother Death will follow you to Earth and bring endless trouble and sadness with him."

Kintu and Nambi quickly gathered their possessions and started their journey to Earth. But at the last moment, Nambi cried out, "I have forgotten grain for the bird! It will die if I do not go back for it!" "You heard your father!" protested Kintu. "If you return, your brother Death will find you and come with us to Earth."

But Nambi did not listen and returned for the grain. And, as Gulu had predicted, Death followed the newlyweds to Earth.

Things went well for a time, but one day Death sent a message to Kintu: "I need a cook. Send me your daughter." "No," replied Kintu. "You will only kill her." Soon after, Death sent another message: "I need a cook. Send me your son." Again, Kintu refused.

In reply, Death melted into the ground. To this day, Death remains on Earth, springing up from the ground to kill Kintu's children as he wishes.

The World of THE GANDA

The Ganda (GAN dah) are one of the largest ethnic groups in the African nation of Uganda. They make up about 20 percent of the country's population. Most Ganda, also known as Baganda (buh GAN duh), live in an area of central and southern Uganda called Buganda (boo GAHN duh).

Ronald Muwenda Mutebi II is crowned as the 36th *Kabaka* (king) of Buganda in 1993. The kingdom of Buganda grew in size and importance in the 1600's and 1700's. By the mid-1800's, it had become one of the richest and most powerful kingdoms in East Africa. In 1894, the United Kingdom made Buganda a British *protectorate* (partially controlled country). In 1896, the British added several other kingdoms to the protectorate, extending it over most of present-day Uganda. However, the Ganda kept their own Kabaka and Lukiko (parliament). Although Uganda became independent in 1962, the country's new constitution allowed Buganda to keep its Kabaka and remain partly independent.

THE MARRIAGE TEST

The "marriage test" is a common *motif* (theme) in myths. Typically, a powerful father tests the worthiness of a young man to marry his daughter. When a young man seeks the hand of a god's daughter, he must prove himself worthy to be the founder of a great people. The Ganda believed that Kintu (kihn too) not only founded the Ganda people but also introduced such culturally important practices as farming.

THE SPIRIT WORLD

Traditional African religions do not draw a line between the physical and spirit worlds. They see them as blending seamlessly. Spirits influence events for good or bad. Most spirits are hostile and must be appeased with offerings. The guardian spirits that feature in traditional beliefs are not always reliable. Individuals must rely on their own efforts as much as aid from the spirit realm. One local proverb says, "Pray for deliverance from danger, but start running, too."

The Ganda believe that Kintu introduced farming to Earth. In the past, the Ganda grew food to support their families, including cassava and sweet potatoes, millet, corn (maize), beans, and bananas. (The thick root of the cassava plant is eaten as food.) Today they also grow crops to sell, even exporting them. Farmers cooperate to grow these "cash crops" on a large scale. The crops include coffee, cotton, tea, and tobacco.

A Ganda woman carries bananas to market in the Buikwe region of Uganda. African women often carry firewood, buckets of water, or farm produce on their head, an efficient means of transport. Although Ganda women play an important role in farming, they have few rights compared with men. If a woman dies, her husband inherits her property. But laws and custom often prevent widows from inheriting their family's property.

LEZA and the Honeyguide

This story of Mayimba the honeyguide
from the Kaonde people offers a
cautionary tale about the dangers
of curiosity.

After the great god, Leza (lay zah), had created Mulonga (moo LAHN guh), the first man, and Mwinambuzhi (mwin am boo zhee), the first woman, he called Mayimba (may yihm buh), the honeyguide, to him.

"Carry these three gourds to the man and woman I created," said Leza. "Inside the first gourd are many seeds. Tell them to plant the seeds from the first gourd so they may have food to eat. But they must not open the other two gourds until I come. Then I will show them what to do with the contents of those two gourds."

Mayimba began the long journey from heaven to Earth. But as he flew, he wondered and wondered, "What fills the other two gourds?"

Eventually the honeyguide could no longer bear his curiosity. He stopped to open the gourds. The first gourd held seeds, as Leza had said. Mayimba put the seeds back in the gourd and plugged the hole just as he found it.

He opened the second gourd. Inside were medicines for healing sickness. But Mayimba could not figure out what they were because sickness and death were unknown. So he put the medicines back in the second gourd and plugged the hole just as he found it.

Then the honeyguide opened the third gourd. Death and disease rushed out in every direction! Frantically, Mayimba tried to catch them to put them back in the third gourd. But he could not.

When Leza at last came to visit Mulonga and Mwinambuzhi, he discovered what the honeyguide had done. "Mayimba has done you a great wrong!" Leza declared to the man and woman. Try as they might, Leza and the bird could not find and capture the evils that had escaped from the third gourd.

Mayimba was afraid that Leza or the people might punish him for his foolishness. So he flew off into the wilderness and no longer lived in the village with his friends.

The World of THE KAONDE

The Kaonde are a farming people who have lived in the northwestern section of what is now Zambia since the 1500's and 1600's. Many Kaonde are Christians, but traditional local beliefs still have a strong hold on the village people.

THE HONEYGUIDE

Honeyguides live up to their name by uttering cries that direct humans and *ratels* (badgerlike animals) to honeybees' nests. After the honey has been harvested, the honeyguide swoops in to devour the bee *larvae* (undeveloped forms) and honeycomb. The honeyguide is a seemingly small and insignificant bird. Thus, it embodies those who succeed through industry and cleverness rather than through strength.

Many Kaonde live in traditional villages of mud huts roofed with straw.

The Kaonde build canoes for traveling on lakes and rivers. They hollow out the trunk of a tree to make a narrow vessel with a flat bottom. Dreaming about a canoe is supposed to be a sign of good luck.

A Kaonde boy looks after his family's oxen. Children in Kaonde villages are expected to help their families by doing many household chores, including fetching water, gathering firewood, and tending and harvesting crops in the fields.

Two Kaonde women greet one another in the street. The Kaonde have a set manner for greetings, and it is considered very rude to start a conversation without first going through the procedure. People first ask about one another's health and then about one another's family, crops, or business. A special greeting for an elder includes dropping to one knee, bowing, and clapping three times. Elders are addressed with special terms that show respect for their age.

DEITIES OF AFRICA

Agemo (ah GEH maw) the Chameleon

Agemo the Chameleon is an *orisha* (lesser god) who helps the Yoruba god Olorun defeat Olokun, the goddess of the sea.

Aja

Aja the Dog is an *orisha* (lesser god) known for his cleverness. But he is also lazy and deceitful and so provides an example of how not to behave.

Ajapa

Ajapa the Tortoise is an *orisha* (lesser god) known for his greed. Like Aja the Dog, Ajapa provides an example of how not to behave.

Anansi (uh NAHN see)

The popular trickster god of West African legend, "Mr. Spider" or "Aunt Nancy," as he is often known, is a constant mischief-maker. Anansi is also popular in parts of the Americas, where he was introduced by African slaves.

Chukwu (CHOOK woo)

The supreme god of the Igbo people, Chukwu, "the great spirit," deals kindly with his people and never wrongs them. Some trees are associated with him and so they are considered to be sacred.

Gulu (goo loo)

Gulu is the Great God of the Ganda people. He and his sons require Kintu, a man, to perform a number of challenging tasks before he is allowed to marry Nambi, Gulu's daughter.

Leza (lay zah)

The great god of the Kaonde people, Leza entrusted his honeyguide messenger to deliver three gourds to the first people. But the honeyguide opened the third, releasing death, sickness, and dangerous animals into the world. Leza was so enraged that he returned to heaven. The Kaonde believe his grumbling causes thunder.

Maori (MOW ree)

The patient Zimbabwean god Maori became fed up with the complaints of the first human, Mwuetsi, and went back to the heavens to live in peace.

Mwuetsi

Originally the Moon, Mwuetsi became the first man after he complained to Maori, the supreme god who created him, about having to live at the bottom of the ocean. Mweutsi and his wives, Massassi (muh SAHS see) and Marongo (muh RAHNG goh), created all people, plants, and animals on Earth. But Maori punished Mweutsi with death after Mweutsi refused to stop creating more and more people.

Nambi (nam bee)

The daughter of Gulu, the Great God of the Ganda (GAN duh) people, Nambi became a bee to help her lover Kintu (kihn too) perform the final task he had to accomplish to win her hand in marriage.

Obatala (ah BAH tah lah)

Obatala was one of the sons of Olorun (oh loh ROON), the Lord God of the Yoruba (YOH ru bah) people. Obatala decided that an Earth with no land was boring. With the help of his brother Orunmilla (oh RUHN mee lah), Obatala made land on Earth for spirits and living things and established the holy city of Ife.

Olodumare

One part of the three-part supreme god in Yoruba mythology, Olodumare is the Creator God. The other parts of this trinity are Olorun, the chief deity, and Olofi, who communicates prayers to heaven and the will of Olorun to Earth.

Olofi

Olofi is one part of a three-part god in Yoruba mythology. He communicates prayers to heaven and the will of Olorun to Earth. The other members of this trinity are Olodumare the Creator God and Olorun, the chief deity.

Olokun (OH loh koon)

Goddess of the sea in Yoruba legend, Olokun was annoyed by Olorun and Obatala's creation of land on Earth. She challenged Olorun's power but was defeated when Agemo the Chameleon tricked her.

Olorun (oh loh ROON)

Olorun, the chief deity in Yoruba mythology, is one part of a three-part god. The other members of this trinity are Olodumare the Creator God and Olofi, who communicates prayers to heaven and the will of Olorun to Earth.

An image of the orisha Shango crowns a staff carried by followers of this lesser god of thunder and lightning during ceremonial dances.

Orishas (oh REE shuhz)

The orishas are a group of lesser gods who are important in the Yoruba pantheon, despite once having tried to dethrone Olorun. They are also worshiped as far away from Africa as the West Indies.

Orunmilla (oh RUHN mee lah)

Known as "One Who Knows Who Will Prosper," Orunmilla is a son of Olorun, the Lord God of the Yoruba. He helps his brother Obatala create land on Earth.

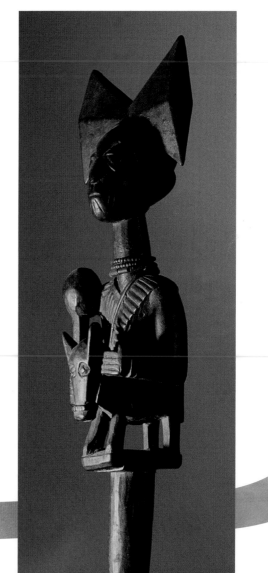

GLOSSARY

constellation A group of stars that form an identifiable pattern, such as an animal or a mythological figure.

creation The process by which the universe was brought into being at the start of time.

creator god In myth, a creator god is one who creates the universe or the earth, geographical features, and often all humans or a particular culture. Creation myths often explain the origin of the world by describing actions that take place in a world that already exists.

deity A god or goddess.

divination Using supernatural means to learn about the future.

gourd A large fruit with a hard body that can be hollowed out and used as a container.

kente cloth A ceremonial cloth with geometric designs made by the Ashanti people of Ghana.

lute A long-necked musical instrument with strings which are plucked to make sounds.

myth A story that a people tell to explain their origins or the origins of natural and social phenomena. Myths often involve gods, spirits, and other supernatural beings.

oba A local chief in Nigeria.

orisha A lesser god in southern Nigeria.

polygamy The practice of having more than one wife at a time.

ritual A solemn religious ceremony in which a set of actions are peformed in a specific order.

sacred Something that is connected with the gods or goddesses and so should be treated with respectful worship.

sacrifice An offering made to a god or gods, often in the form of an animal or even a person who is killed for the purpose. Sacrifices also take the shape of valued possessions that might be buried, placed in caves, or thrown into a lake for the gods.

scarification To create a ritual design on the skin by making a series of cuts.

seer A person who is believed to have the power to foresee or foretell future events.

shaman A person who enters a trance during a religious ritual to gain access to the world of the spirits. In many cultures, a shaman is seen as an intermediary between humans and the spiritual world.

suitor A man who aims to marry a particular woman.

supernatural Describes something that cannot be explained by science or by the laws of nature, which is therefore said to be caused by beings such as gods, spirits, or ghosts.

taboo A social or religious custom that prohibits a particular practice, such as eating particular foods.

trickster A supernatural figure who engages in mischievous activities that either benefit or harm humans. The motives behind a trickster's behavior are not always clear. Tricksters appear in various shapes in myths around the world, including Coyote and Raven in Native American cultures.

tuber A thick, enlarged portion of a stem that usually grows underground. Potatoes, Jerusalem artichokes, and yams are examples of tubers.

FOR FURTHER INFORMATION

Books

Abrahams, Roger D. (ed.). *African Folk Tales* (The Pantheon Fairy Tale and Folklore Library). Pantheon, 1999.

Allan, Tony, Fergus Fleming, and Charles Phillips. *African Beliefs and Mythologies* (World Mythologies). Rosen Publishing Group, 2012.

Arnott, Kathleen. *Tales from Africa* (Oxford Myths and Legends). Oxford University Press, 2000.

Chambers, Catherine. *African Myths and Legends* (All About Myths). Raintree, 2013.

Fredericks, Anthony D. *African Legends, Myths, and Folktales for Readers Theatre.* Teachers Ideas Press, 2008.

Green, Jen. *West African Myths* (Myths from Around the World). Gareth Stevens Publishing, 2010.

Hibbert, Claire. *Terrible Tales of Africa* (Monstrous Myths). Gareth Stevens Publishing, 2014.

Jeffrey, Gary. *African Myths* (Graphic Mythology). Rosen Publishing Group, 2006.

Lynch, Patricia Ann, and Jeremy Roberts. *African Mythology A to Z.* Chelsea House Publishers, 2010.

National Geographic Essential Visual History of World Mythology. National Geographic Society, 2008.

Philip, Neil. *Eyewitness Mythology* (DK Eyewitness Books). DK Publishing, 2011.

Quigley, Mary. *Ancient West African Kingdoms: Ghana, Mali, and Songhai* (Understanding People in the Past). Heinemann, 2002.

Richardson, Hazel. *Life in Ancient Africa* (Peoples of the Ancient World). Crabtree Publishing Company, 2005.

Schomp, Virginia, *The Ancient Africans* (Myths of the World). Marshall Cavendish Benchmark Books, 2009.

Sheehan, Sean. *Ancient African Kingdoms* (Exploring the Ancient World). Gareth Stevens Publishing, 2010.

Woodson, Carter Godwin. *African Myths and Folk Tales* (Dover Children's Thrift Classics). Dover Publications, 2010.

Websites

http://www.godchecker.com/pantheon /african-mythology.php
A directory of African deities from God Checker, written in a light-hearted style but with accurate information.

http://www.pantheon.org/areas /mythology/africa/african/
Encyclopedia Mythica page with links to many pages about myths from different African cultures.

http://www.mythencyclopedia.com /A-Am/African-Mythology.html
This Myth Encyclopedia entry is a discussion of various aspects of African mythology.

http://www.rmg.co.uk/explore/astronomy- and-time/astronomy-facts/stars/south- africa-stars-myths.
The website for the Royal Museums Greenwich has an article on South African star myths.

http://www.agallery.de/docs/mythology.htm
A directory of gods and themes from African mythology on a page dedicated to contemporary African painting.

INDEX

PRONUNCIATION KEY

Sound	As in
a	hat, map
ah	father, far
ai	care, air
aw	order
aw	all
ay	age, face
ch	child, much
ee	equal, see
ee	machine, city
eh	let, best
ih	it, pin, hymn
k	coat, look
o	hot, rock
oh	open, go
oh	grow, tableau
oo	rule, move, food
ow	house, out
oy	oil, voice
s	say, nice
sh	she, abolition
u	full, put
u	wood
uh	cup, butter
uh	flood
uh	about, ameba
uh	taken, purple
uh	pencil
uh	lemon
uh	circus
uh	labyrinth
uh	curtain
uh	Egyptian
uh	section
uh	fabulous
ur	term, learn, sir, work
y	icon, ice, five
yoo	music
zh	pleasure